THIS BOOK BELONGS TO

children's choice®

BENJY
and
The Barking Bird

Margaret Bloy Graham

Harper & Row, Publishers   New York,

Benjy was a brown dog with long ears and a short tail.

He loved everybody in his family—Mother, Father,

Linda, and Jimmy—and they all loved him.

He was a happy dog until he heard the words,

"Tomorrow Aunt Sarah is coming for a visit,

and she's bringing Tilly."

Tilly was Aunt Sarah's parrot. When Tilly was there,

Benjy's family always fussed over her and never paid

any attention to him. That made Benjy jealous.

The moment Aunt Sarah arrived she said,

"Come on, Tilly, show them your new trick.

Say *bow wow*, sweetheart."

"BOW WOW! BOW WOW!" squawked Tilly.

"Gee," said Jimmy, "Tilly can bark better than Benjy."

Benjy couldn't stand it. He went out into the backyard.

He decided not to come into the house again
until that awful parrot had gone. He could still hear her:
"BOW WOW! BOW WOW! BOW WOW!"
Tilly barked so long and so loud that all the dogs

in the neighborhood came running.

Soon the backyard was full of barking dogs.

They made so much noise that Benjy's ears hurt.

Father came to the door and shouted, "Get out of here!"

"For goodness' sake, be quiet, Tilly!" said Aunt Sarah.

"I don't know what's got into that bird.

She's been contrary all spring."

"Linda dear," said Mother,

"put Tilly up in Aunt Sarah's room

so we can have peace and quiet for lunch."

Benjy was still outside, more jealous than ever.
Suddenly he had an idea. While the family was chatting
at lunch, he sneaked into the house,
past the dining room, and up to Aunt Sarah's room.
Tilly was asleep, tired out from her barking.

Carefully Benjy picked up her cage

and brought it out into the backyard.

He was just lifting it into the trash barrel

when the handle of the cage door caught on the edge.

The door sprang open and Tilly escaped!

Off she flew to the big maple tree, right into a flock

of sparrows. In a flash Tilly and the sparrows flew away.

Benjy just stood there, stunned.

Then all at once he felt happy. Tilly was gone!

Quickly he hid the cage in the trash barrel and ran into the house.

After lunch Aunt Sarah
went to her room.
Right away she ran out
screaming, "Tilly's gone!"
Everyone began
talking at once:
"Impossible!" "No!"
"Where did she go?"
Finally Father said,
"Don't worry.
We'll find her."

So the whole family set out to look for Tilly—

except Aunt Sarah.
She was too upset to go.
She even began to cry.
Benjy was watching her.
He'd been so happy
that Tilly was gone—
now he felt miserable.
He'd rather have her back.

Maybe she *had* come back. He ran to the maple tree, but no Tilly.
He looked for her everywhere, but no Tilly. All he could see
were a few sparrows flying around the roof of the house.

Meanwhile the family searched for Tilly all over town,
but they could not find her.

"It's getting late," Father said finally. "Let's go home.
We'll put an ad in the paper tonight. Tomorrow
we'll start out early and take Benjy with us."

Next morning when everyone was having breakfast,

Benjy ran in barking furiously. "Stop it, Benjy," said Mother.

"You'll remind Aunt Sarah of Tilly."

But Benjy kept on barking. Then he ran up the stairs.

"Go and see what he's up to, children," said Father.

The children ran after Benjy. "Father! Mother!"
they called from the attic. "Come quick!"
Father, Mother, and Aunt Sarah dashed up.
There was Benjy barking at the window...

and there was Tilly right outside!

She was flying around with a twig in her beak.

"Tilly," cried Aunt Sarah. "What *are* you doing?"

"She's helping a sparrow build a nest," said Linda.

"That's what birds do in the spring."

"She never did *that* before," said Aunt Sarah. "Tilly,
please come in." Aunt Sarah tried and tried to get Tilly
to come inside. She tried with sunflower seeds,
hard-boiled eggs, apples, and coaxing.
But it was no use. Tilly did not pay any attention.

She and the sparrow kept bringing more and more twigs
and pieces of string. There was now a big nest
under the eaves. "We'll have to ask the Fire Department
to catch Tilly," said Father. In all the excitement
nobody noticed that Benjy had disappeared.

An hour later the phone rang.

It was Mr. Jones, the man from the pet store.

"Your little dog is here," he said, "and he won't go home."

"I'll send the children to get him," said Father.

When Linda and Jimmy got to the pet store,

there was Benjy, staring up at a parrot.

"I don't know why," said Mr. Jones,

"but he keeps looking at Sparky.

He seems to want that parrot."

"I bet I know why Benjy wants him," said Jimmy.

"Me too," said Linda. "Please, Mr. Jones, let us take Sparky home."

Meanwhile the ladder truck of the Fire Department had arrived.

The ladder was being raised to the attic window.

A fireman with a net climbed up. "Here, Tilly! Here, Tilly!"
he called. The grown-ups watched eagerly. No one had noticed
that the children were back with Benjy and Sparky—

no one, that is, except Tilly. From the roof
she made a beeline for Sparky's cage, sat in front of it,
and cooed and cooed. It was love at first sight!

Linda opened the cage door and Tilly flew straight in.

"Why, Tilly's been lonely," said Aunt Sarah.

"I never thought of that. How wonderful you children were to get her a friend!"

"That was Benjy's idea," said Jimmy.

Then everyone began talking at once:

"How clever he is!" "A real bird dog!" "Almost human!"

Benjy just stood there wagging his tail.

Next spring when Aunt Sarah came for a visit,

she came alone. "I left Tilly and Sparky

with a bird-sitter," she said. "They're so happy together.

"Look what I brought you," she went on,

and she pulled out a photograph.

"That's Tilly sitting on an egg!"

"Show it to Benjy too," said Jimmy.

"Of course," said Aunt Sarah.

"Why, Benjy's the one who started it all."

This time Benjy really enjoyed Aunt Sarah's visit.
She took him for a walk every day and always
bought him a special snack at the butcher's.
And from then on, Benjy was Aunt Sarah's favorite dog,
and Aunt Sarah was Benjy's favorite aunt.